D1133031

nina h.

The illustrations for this book were created with pencil, ink, and watercolor paints.

Copyright © 2014 by Nina Huang · All rights reserved. No part of this book may be used, reproduced, distributed, or transmitted in any manner whatsoever without the written permission of the publisher, except in the case of brief quotations for articles or reviews ·
Published by Nina Huang Art Studio, Portland, USA 2014 · Visit our website at www.ninahuangart.com · First edition: January 2014 · Summary: *My Apollo* is about a small boy named Briar and a rescue greyhound dog named Apollo, and how they came together to lend each other a helping hand · ISBN-10: 0-615-94465-5 · ISBN-13: 978-0-615-94465-4 · Printed in China

For Barry, Anthony, Amy, Fion,
and everyone whose life has been changed forever
by the love of an animal.

This winter had been long and difficult for Briar and his dad.

Briar's mom moved out over the summer.

So, this year, there were no birthday pancakes.

No Halloween candy.

And Christmas came and went without any sparkly lights in the house.

On top of that, the school counselor said that Briar was falling behind in his classes, sleeping when he should have been reading, and not playing with others.

On the ride home from school, Dad was really quiet.

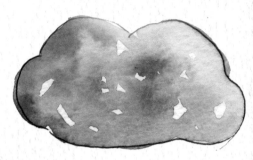

"Wait, this isn't the way home," Briar said. "Where are we going?" Dad smiled and answered, "We're going to make today a good day."

When they finally stopped, it was at a dog shelter! Briar couldn't believe it—he had been begging his dad for a dog forever.

"This is a shelter for greyhounds," Dad said. "They are bred to run races so people can place bets and make money. But when they get older and slower, they're given away and need to find forever homes, and it's not always easy."

There were so many of them: white ones, black ones, tan ones, and some with stripes like tigers. Dad patted Briar on the head and asked, "So, Briar, who's going to come home with us today?"

How could Briar choose? They were all beautiful animals. He looked and looked, and found a scared greyhound tucked in the back of his crate, shaking.

"His named is Apollo. We think he was abused while he was on the racetrack, but we can't know for sure," the shelter lady said. "Whoever takes him home will need to be extra patient and kind. It will take some time for him to open up."

In that instant Briar knew, this was *his* dog. He understood that Apollo was afraid and sad, and he knew he could help Apollo feel better.

Poor Apollo was scared of so many strange things.
Like passing cars. Loud noises.
Sudden movements.
Cats and mice.

Even the couch! Why would a
dog be scared of a soft, comfy couch?

Most of all, Apollo was afraid of being touched. Sometimes he seemed fine so Briar would try to pet him, but then Apollo would start shaking and backing away.

Dad told Briar that because people had been unkind to Apollo, now he didn't trust them.

"It's a defense mechanism," Dad explained.

Briar hoped that Apollo will trust him soon.

In time, Briar learned that there were things Apollo loved.

Apollo always got very excited and wagged his tail like crazy when Briar took him out for a walk.

Apollo would take the time to smell each and every flower, all the way to the park.

At the park, while other dogs would play fetch, Apollo ran in circles, *really*, *really* fast with a silly grin on his face.

Briar had never ever seen a dog run so fast!

Apollo also loved other dogs at the park, especially greyhounds.

"You've got a greyhound, too!" said a girl with a black greyhound.
"My name is Elli, and this is Emma. Can I pet your dog?" she asked
and reached for Apollo...

"No, no, I'm sorry, but Apollo doesn't like being touched." Briar explained, "We just brought him home not too long ago, and we think maybe somebody was mean to him."

"Emma didn't like being touched when we first brought her home, either," Elli whispered as she stepped away from Apollo, not wanting to scare him.

"Really?" Briar reached and petted Emma on the head. Emma looked up at Briar, all smiles.

"See," Elli giggled. "She's not afraid anymore."

Briar asked, "Can you teach me how to help Apollo?"

So while Apollo and Emma ran around and played, Elli told Briar everything she knew about greyhounds.

She gave him a list of things to do with Apollo to help him not be so scared of people, starting with Briar, his "human dad."

Elli's list of things to try with Apollo

Make Apollo a comfortable bed in your room.

This teaches him that he has a safe place, and that place is with you.

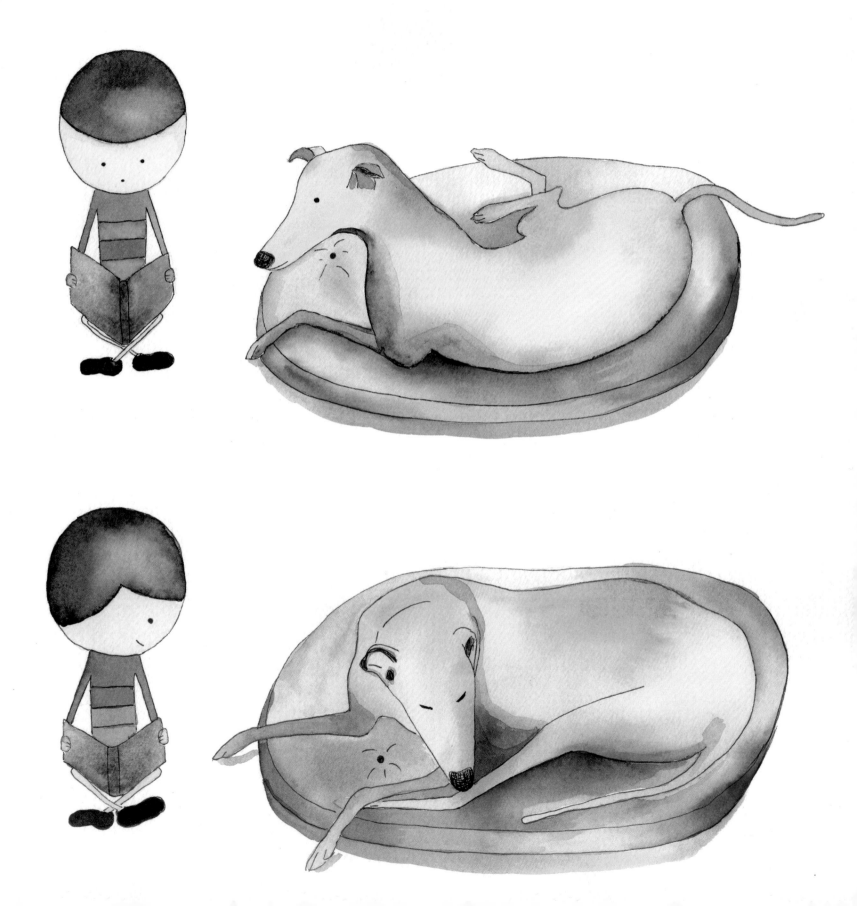

Rain or shine, take Apollo out for his walk at the same time every day. Routine is comforting to dogs, and he will learn to look forward to this time with you.

Every time he comes when you call, give him a treat as a reward.

Giving him rules and new challenges helps him feel stable.

I hope it wasn't my fault that Mom left...

I wish I could help Dad feel better somehow...

I'm worried about school...

Tell Apollo all your secrets.

If you trust him with your open heart, he will trust you back.

Make sure you are the one to feed Apollo every day,
so he knows he can rely on you.

Briar practiced Elli's tips daily, and over time he could see that Apollo was improving. He wasn't even afraid of the couch anymore.

And when Briar finally reached his hand out to pet Apollo, he was fine!

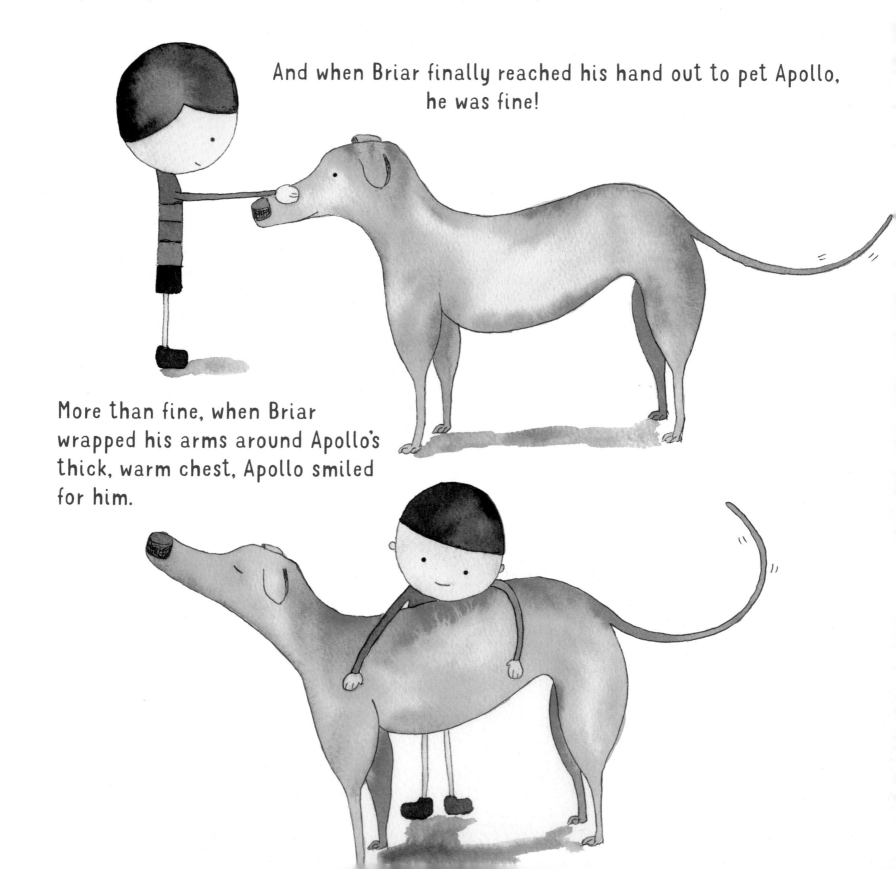

More than fine, when Briar wrapped his arms around Apollo's thick, warm chest, Apollo smiled for him.

One night Dad came home late, and the house was still.
When Briar and Apollo didn't come greet him, he went to
check on them in Briar's room.

They had fallen asleep together on Apollo's fluffy bed.

They looked so content, Dad just laid a blanket on top
of them and let them be.

Briar woke up the next morning like a bolt of lightning. He was so eager for the big day of playing ahead of him with Elli, Emma, and Apollo.

"Where are you rushing to? It's Saturday." Dad asked.

"I'm meeting my friends at the park! I told you already!" Briar replid, looking everywhere for Apollo's leash... which Apollo had been holding in his mouth the whole time.

Dad laughed and kissed Briar on the forehead, and then Apollo.

"You boys have fun. When you get back, there'll be pancakes!"

The End

The publication of *My Apollo* was made possible by our gracious and generous contributors:

Scott Abrams· Donna Alexander · Sherry Alexander · C. Scott Ananian · Ellen Banta
Dave Conrey · Caitlin Daniel · Shirley Decker · the Deterding Family · Dolce Gambino
Craig Holt · Sam Howard · Bobby Huang · Amy Huang · Anthony Huang · Tonya Kong
Kevin Lewis · Sara Lindberg · Diane E Mefford · Amy Montanus · Vicki Maisano
Laura Pellegrini · Mark Ratzlaff · Shannon Roche · Matt Angron Ross · Charan Sethi
Lili Shintani · Barbara Smith · Rand Stamm· Barbara Stanley · Rafael Susana
Sonya Swankier · Trish Titer · Acey Toothypegs · Dianne West · Barry Williams

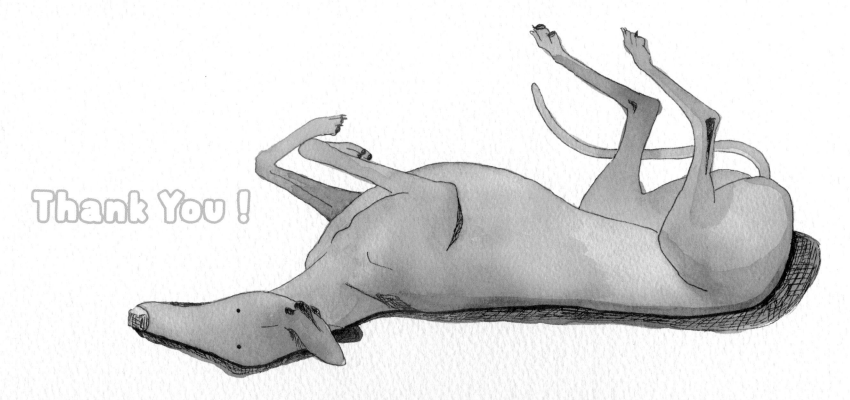

Thank You !